JODY

DONNA TODD

For Madeleine
Illustrated by Michael Garland

Copyright © 1989, 1980 by George Shea.
All rights reserved. Published by Scholastic Inc.
SPRINT and SPRINT BOOKS are trademarks of Scholastic Inc.
Printed in the U.S.A.
ISBN 0-590-35157-5

6 7 8 9 10   31   03 02 01 00 99 98

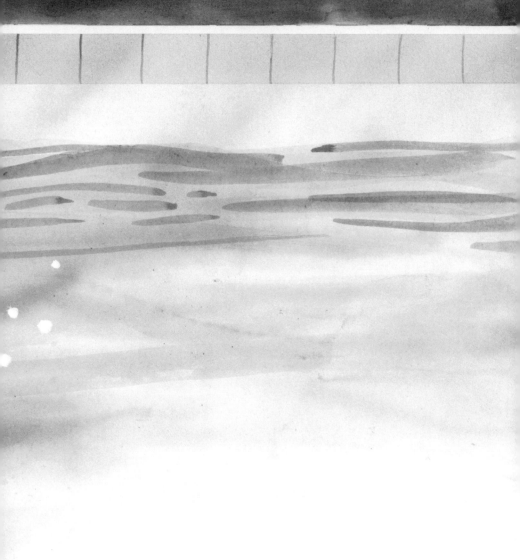

CHAPTER 1

Jody was scared the moment she saw the pool. It looked deep and green.

Suddenly, she was at the bottom of it. The cold water had closed over her head. She could not breathe.

She was sure she was going to drown. There was nothing she could do.

Just then, Jody woke up. She looked around and saw that she was in her own room. She had only been dreaming. But she still felt afraid.

school. The bell rang for gym class. She went to her locker. She started to change into her shorts.

"Where is your swim suit?" asked the girl next to her.

"I don't have one," answered Jody.

"You don't!" said the girl. "Everyone swims around here. That's what we do in gym class. We swim."

"I don't," said Jody. "I don't like the water. I guess I'm . . . a little afraid of it."

"Well, you'd better get over that," said the

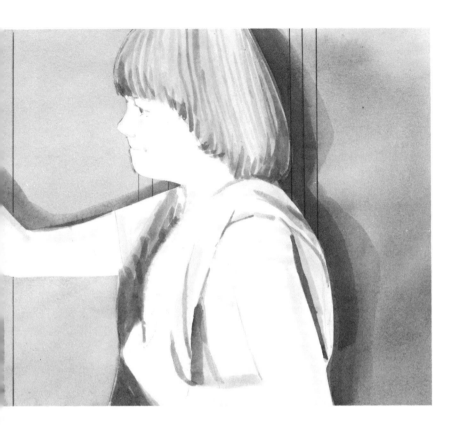

girl. "Swimming is a big thing in this school. That's why we have a pool. What's your name?"

"Jody."

"I'm Sandy," the girl said. "I'm captain of the swimming team. I keep an extra swim suit here in my locker. You can use it."

Jody wanted to say no. But Sandy didn't give her a chance. She quickly took out the swim suit and handed it to Jody.

Jody put on the swim suit. Then she and the others headed for the pool.

CHAPTER 2

As soon as Jody got close to the pool, she felt afraid. The pool was deep and green. It was just like the pool in her dream.

Ms. Ryder, the gym teacher, spoke to the class. "We are not going in right away. I want you all to sit down at the shallow end."

The water was not deep there. Jody sat on the edge. She sat between Sandy and a girl called Carol.

"Sandy says you're afraid of the water," said Carol.

"I guess I am . . . a little," said Jody.

"We can help you get over it," said Carol.

Suddenly, the two girls pushed Jody from behind. Jody fell into the pool.

The water was not deep. But her fear made her helpless. She could not stand up.

Water filled her nose and mouth. She could not breathe. Suddenly, she was grabbed from behind. It was Ms. Ryder. She picked Jody up. After a few minutes, Jody was all right.

The teacher looked down at her. "How did this happen?" she asked.

"Some kids pushed me in," said Jody. "I . . . I can't swim."

"Who were they?" the teacher asked.

Jody didn't want to get Sandy and Carol into trouble. That would be a bad way to start out at a new school.

"I don't know who it was," Jody answered.

"Yes, you do," said Ms. Ryder. "I want to know."

Everyone in the room looked at Jody. They were all waiting to hear what she would say. Jody took a deep breath.

"I want to know," Ms. Ryder said again. "Who pushed you?"

"It was those two there," said Jody. She pointed out Sandy and Carol.

CHAPTER 3

When the class ended, Jody went back to her locker. Suddenly, Sandy and Carol were standing right beside her.

"Too bad you can't keep your mouth closed," said Sandy.

"The water wasn't even deep," Carol said.

"We're in trouble now," said Sandy. "So we're going to make trouble for you, too."

"I can handle trouble," Jody said. "What do you have in mind?"

"You'll see," said Sandy. Then she and Carol walked away.

Later that day, Jody went to the lunch room. She sat down beside some kids from her class. "Hi," she said.

No one answered her. They all acted as if Jody were not there.

For days no one spoke to Jody. Sandy and Carol were doing a good job of getting even.

One afternoon after class, Sandy walked up to Jody. "Ms. Ryder wants to see you," she said. Then she turned and walked away.

Jody headed for Ms. Ryder's office. It was next to the pool. As she walked past the pool, she heard a scream.

She ran to the pool. She saw a girl from her class in the water. She was moving her arms and legs. "Help!" the girl screamed. "Help me!"

Suddenly, Jody was sick with fear. She ran
into the locker room. "Help!" she screamed.

She beat on the door of Ms. Ryder's office. But
there was no answer.

Suddenly, Sandy and Carol came along. They were with some kids from Jody's class.

"The pool!" Jody yelled. "Someone is drowning in there!"

They all started to run out of the locker room. Jody could not believe what she saw next.

The drowning girl was standing at the door. She smiled and waved. "Hi," she called out.

"Hi, Jane!" said Sandy. Then they all began to laugh.

Suddenly Jody knew. The whole thing was a trick, a joke. She was angry. "Go on — laugh!" she yelled. Then she began to cry. She turned and started to run away.

"Wait!" called the girl who had pretended to be drowning. "I'm sorry — "

But Jody was gone.

That night, there was a knock at Jody's door. A girl stood at the door. It was the one who had pretended to be drowning.

"What do you want?" asked Jody. "Is this another joke?"

"No," said the girl. "My name is Jane Capra. I'm sorry about what happened today. Sandy and Carol talked me into it."

"I hope you all had fun," said Jody.

"Listen," said Jane. "I don't like what they're doing to you. I want to be your friend."

Jody didn't say anything.

"A group of us are going to the lake tomorrow," Jane said. "Would you like to come? You could meet some of the other kids."

Jody wanted to say yes. But she wondered if it was just another trick. "All right," she said finally. "I'll go."

CHAPTER 4

The next day was Saturday. Jody met Jane and her friends in the afternoon. They all went to the lake.

Sandy and Carol were at the lake waiting for

them. Jody felt she had been tricked again.

"Let's go swimming!" yelled Sandy.

"Come on," said Jane. "Let's go in the water. I'll swim with you. You don't have to go near the deep part."

"No, thanks," said Jody. She didn't trust Jane now. She didn't trust any of them. She was not going to go near the water.

Jody watched as they all went in. They all came out again after a while. Only Jane stayed in.

Jody thought of going home. Then she looked up and saw Jane's head come up out of the water. Her eyes were wide open. She seemed to be reaching for air. She was not in deep water. But she looked as if she was in trouble.

Jody ran over to Sandy and Carol and the others. "I think Jane's in trouble," she said.

"Sure," said Sandy, laughing. "Jane is only a great swimmer."

"You're a good swimmer," said Carol. "Jump in and save her." They all laughed.

Jody ran down to the edge of the lake. There was no sign of Jane now.

Was it another joke? She could still hear the other girls laughing.

Just then, Jody saw a hand come out of the water. Quickly, Jody took a deep breath. Then she headed into the water.

CHAPTER 5

Jody went in deeper with each step. Soon the water was up to her waist. She was afraid to go any farther.

Jody turned and called to the kids on the shore. "Somebody help me!" she yelled.

One of the girls started to go toward the water. "Stay here!" yelled Carol. "Don't be stupid! Jane is only kidding around!"

Suddenly, Jane's head came up out of the water. Her eyes were wide with fear. She could not stay up. She went down under again.

Jody knew she could not wait a second longer. She took a deep breath and went under.

Jody felt for Jane's arm. She found it and stood up. She pulled Jane up with her. Jane couldn't stand up. Jody put her hands under Jane's arms and pulled her to shore.

"Thanks, Jody," Jane said. "I couldn't stand up. I got cramps in my legs and couldn't move them. Then I swallowed some water."

Carol, Sandy, and the others crowded around.

Jody became angry. "Jane was not just fooling around!" she yelled. "She almost drowned!"

Sandy and Carol just stood there. They did not know what to say.

"I almost drowned once when I was little," Jody told them.

"Is that why you're so afraid of the water?" asked Jane.

Jody thought for a moment. She pushed her wet hair from her eyes. Then she said with a smile, "Yes. But I'm not so afraid anymore."